DISASTER ALERT!

Environmental Disaster Alert!

Paul Challen

Crabtree Publishing Company
www.crabtreebooks.com

presented by:

Crabtree Publishing Company
www.crabtreebooks.com

For Sam, Evelina, and Henry

Coordinating editor: Ellen Rodger

Project editor: Carrie Gleason

Indexer and proofreader: Sean Charlebois

Book design and production coordinator: Rosie Gowsell

Cover design: Rob MacGregor

Photo research: Allison Napier

Consultant: Dr. Hans Tammemagi, Environmental Consultant

Photographs: Ainaco/ CORBIS: p. 5; APWide World Photos: p. 4 (bottom), p. 9 (top left), p. 15 (bottom), p. 16 (bottom), p. 19 (top), p. 20 (middle), p. 23 (bottom); Baldev/ CORBIS/ SYGMA: p. 14 (inset); Bettman/ CORBIS: p. 8 (bottom right), p. 18 (top); Jonathon Blair/ CORBIS: p. 24 (top); Mark Boulton/ Photo Researchers, Inc: p. 22 (bottom); Cooperphoto/ CORBIS: p. 10 (top left); Natalie Fobes/ CORBIS: p. 25 (bottom); Simon Frazer/ Photo Researchers, Inc: p. 25 (top); Martin Harvey/ CORBIS: p. 8 (top left); Matt Herron/ Mira.com: cover; Fred Hoogervorst/ Panos Pictures: p. 29 (bottom); Hulton-Deutsch Collection/ CORBIS: p. 19 (bottom); Rod Johnson/ Panos Pictures: p. 14 (middle); Journal-Courier/ The Image Works: p. 9 (top right); Los Alamos National Library/ Photo Researchers, Inc: p. 3; Paul Lowe/ Panos Pictures: p. 21 (top); Enrique Marcarian/ Reuters: p. 20 (top and bottom); Wally McNamee/ CORBIS: p. 17 (bottom); Roy Morch/ CORBIS: p. 7 (middle); T. Nilson/ Jvz/ Photo Researchers, Inc: p. 7 (top); North Wind/ North Wind Picture Archives: p. 17 (top); Novosti/ Science Photo Library: p. 15 (inset); Gabe Palmer/ CORBIS: p. 26 (bottom); Photolink/ Getty Images: p. 16 (top); David Pollack/ CORBIS: p. 10 (top right); Topham/ The Image Works: p. 27 (bottom); Vanessa Vick/ Photo Researchers, Inc: p. 24 (bottom); Alison Wright/ CORBIS: p. 28; E. Younng/ Photo Researchers, Inc: p. 21 (bottom); John Zoiner/ CORBIS: p. 26 (top)

Illustrations: Robert MacGregor: p. 28; Dan Pressman: p. 6, p. 11, p. 13 (all); David Wysotski, Allure Illustrations: pp. 30-31

Cover: An oil drilling platform on fire in the Gulf of Mexico pollutes the air and water.

Contents: Atomic bombs release harmful radiation into the atmosphere when they are detonated. Since 1963, atmospheric testing of atomic bombs has been banned. Today, most atomic bombs are tested underground, where radiation can be contained, or by using computer models.

Title page: Garbage thrown into rivers and streams pollutes the water and kills the fish.

Crabtree Publishing Company

www.crabtreebooks.com   1-800-387-7650

Cataloging-in-Publication data

Challen, Paul C. (Paul Clarence), 1967-
    Environmental disaster alert! / written by Paul Challen.
        p. cm. -- (Disaster alert!)
    Includes index.
    ISBN 0-7787-1581-7 (rlb) -- ISBN 0-7787-1613-9 (pbk)
    1. Natural disasters--Juvenile literature. 2. Environmental degradation--Juvenile literature. I. Title. II. Series.
        GB5019.C33 2005
        363.34--dc22
                                        2004013056
                                            LC

**Published in
the United States**
PMB 16A
350 Fifth Ave.
Suite 3308
New York, NY
10118

**Published
in Canada**
616 Welland Ave.,
St. Catharines,
Ontario, Canada
L2M 5V6

**Published in the
United Kingdom**
73 Lime Walk
Headington
Oxford
0X3 7AD
United Kingdom

**Published
in Australia**
386 Mt. Alexander Rd.,
Ascot Vale (Melbourne)
V1C 3032

Table of Contents

Our Precious World

When people think of natural disasters, they usually think of events such as hurricanes, tornadoes, or volcanoes, which are caused by forces humans cannot control. Some of the most serious disasters in nature do not happen by chance, but by the actions of humans.

What is a disaster?
A disaster is a destructive event that affects the natural world and human communities. Some disasters are predictable and others occur without warning. Coping successfully with a disaster depends on a community's preparation.

Balancing the biosphere

Every living thing on our planet relies on air, water, and sunlight as its most basic needs. Animal and plant life exist on a narrow stretch on, just above, and just below, the Earth's surface called the biosphere. All the many forms of life are connected with one another in the biosphere. When one part of the biosphere is thrown off balance by an environmental disaster, the whole system runs into serious problems.

(above) One of the biggest strains on our environment comes from too many people producing too much trash.

(right) The fight of protesters against unsafe environmental practices of companies and governments helps make others aware.

Disaster strikes!

Unfortunately, humans sometimes act in ways that are not harmonious with the environment. An environmental disaster is a human-caused event that brings serious immediate or long-term damage to the planet. Air, land, and water pollution, the destruction of forests by over-cutting, and the use of poisonous **chemicals** to kill pests, are a few of the ways in which humans cause environmental disasters. Some human actions that may appear to be beneficial in the short term, can be very harmful in the long run.

Chemical waste dumped from factories into streams and rivers pollutes our water supply.

Corn maidens

Many cultures around the world have traditionally believed that the environment was controlled by spirits that existed in harmony with people. When humans treated the Earth with care, the spirits rewarded people, but when people treated nature poorly, the spirits made life on Earth very difficult. In one legend, the Zuni, who live in the southwestern United States, were punished by mythical figures called Corn Maidens, for taking the harvest for granted. The Corn Maidens brought severe drought upon the Zuni for not taking proper care of their land and crops.

Protect the environment

Through the work of scientists and **environmental organizations**, people are now beginning to understand that their actions have a serious impact on life on this planet. By learning about how environmental disasters occur, and how human actions cause them, people can go a long way towards preventing them.

Water Supply

Water is one of the most important parts of our environment. Humans, plants, and animals all need water to survive. Water pollution occurs when a foreign material or substance is poured directly into a body of water, such as oil during an oil spill. Water pollution can also be caused indirectly, by chemicals or waste entering the water cycle through the air or soil.

The water cycle

The Earth does not create new water every time it rains or snows. Water moves through the environment in a continuous cycle called the water cycle. The water cycle begins when the sun heats bodies of water, such as the oceans, lakes, and rivers, and even the water droplets on the leaves of plants. Water evaporates, or changes into a gas called water vapor. Water vapor rises into the air, where it cools and forms clouds, in a process called **condensation**. Winds blow clouds high over land, and the water in clouds cools as it rises. Water droplets collect to form precipitation, or rain,

snow, or hail, that fall back to Earth. Water runs into rivers and streams, and some of it soaks through soil and into a layer of rock under the ground, called an aquifer. Farmers use water to irrigate crops, animals and people drink it or bathe in it, and plants take it in through their roots. The water that is not used flows through streams and rivers and into the ocean. The whole water cycle starts again with evaporation.

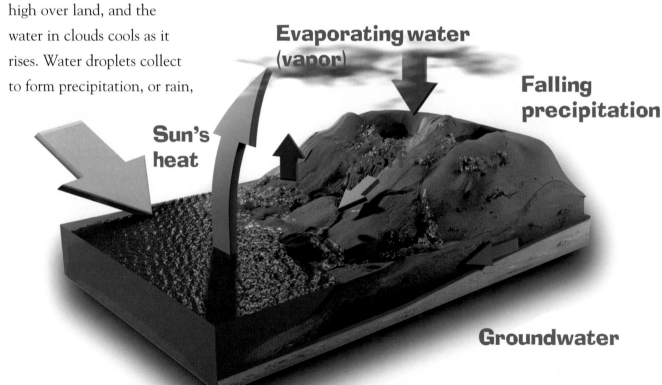

Evaporating water (vapor)

Falling precipitation

Sun's heat

Groundwater

Water pollutants

Pollutants from different sources enter the water cycle in a variety of ways. In some industries, such as manufacturing and mining, waste water containing poisonous chemicals is dumped into lakes or onto the soil. When rain falls on the soil, it **seeps** through the ground, taking the chemicals with it to aquifers. One of the biggest causes of pollution is burning **fossil fuels** to run automobiles, generate electricity, and run machines in factories. Fossil fuels create harmful **waste gases** that rise into the air, mix with water vapor, and fall as **acid rain**.

Drinking polluted water makes people, plants, and animals ill. It also causes **deformities** and **contamination** in animals that live in water, which are passed on to people who eat them.

One effect of burning fossil fuels is the creation of acid rain. When acid rain falls on trees and plants, it can burn the waxy covering on their leaves, stunt their growth, and weaken them.

Dams are large concrete structures built to control the flow of water. Sometimes, a dam will burst, or break. When this happens a sudden flow of water washes over land, the strength of which can wipe out all trees, animals, people, and homes in its path.

7

Oil Spills

Oil spills are one of the most serious and harmful environmental disasters. All around the world's oceans, large ships called tankers and super-tankers transport oil and gas.

On the high seas

Storms, breakdowns in equipment, explosions, collisions with other ships, rocks, and icebergs damage tankers. If the damage to the ship is serious enough, the oil starts to leak out into the water. If the ship's crew cannot quickly block the leak, the oil spreads out on top of the water, causing an oil slick.

Oil in the food chain

Plants and animals that live in the water and on shore are poisoned by the oil that collects on the water's surface. Birds that rely on fish for food die from eating oil-contaminated fish, and from having their feathers coated in oil, which enters their skin and makes it impossible for them to stay warm. People who rely on the fish for their food find the fish too toxic to eat.

Step-by-step

Every oil spill happens in a different way, but there are a few common events that happen in most spills:

STEP 1:
Oil is transported by tanker ships along the surface of a large body of water.

STEP 2:
An accident occurs, ripping a hole in the bottom or sides of the ship.

STEP 3:

Oil leaks from the tanker into the water. On the oceans, the salt in the water helps the oil to float. As the oil slick rapidly spreads out, it forms a thin layer on the water's surface.

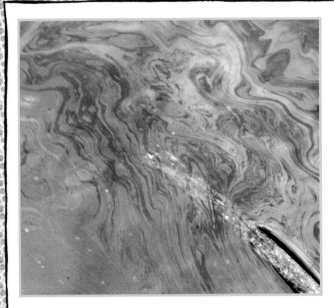

STEP 4:

As the oil slick continues to spread, the layer becomes thinner. By the time the oil has spread to a very thin layer, it is known as a "sheen," and has a rainbow-like appearance.

STEP 5:

Birds, fish, and other animal life swallow the oil-covered water or absorb it through their skin, and marine plants are also killed. In large oil spills, an enormous number of living things die.

The Atmosphere

The layer of air, clouds, and gases that surrounds Earth is called the atmosphere. More than three-quarters of the atmosphere is made up of a gas called nitrogen, and just a little less than a quarter is oxygen, the gas that humans and animals breathe.

A big greenhouse

Within the atmosphere, air, gases, and water vapor are constantly in motion. The gases in the atmosphere cause heat from the sun to stay close to Earth's surface, warming up plants and animals. Gases that cause this warming are called greenhouse gases. Greenhouse gases are primarily made up of a gas called **carbon dioxide**. Carbon dioxide occurs naturally in the atmosphere, but is also created by burning fossil fuels in automobiles and some electrical power plants.

Burning fossil fuels causes more greenhouse gases to be released into the atmosphere, and Earth's temperature is increasing as a result. This is known as global warming. Global warming does not affect the average yearly temperature on Earth very much. Scientists believe that global warming will have serious long term effects, such as the melting of ice at the north and south poles, making water levels around the world rise. This will lead to floods being more common all over the world.

Coal burning power plants create electricity. Unfortunately, burning the fossil fuel also creates harmful waste gases that not only affect global warming, but also cause breathing and other health problems in people.

Layer upon layer

Scientists have divided the atmosphere into five layers: the troposphere, the stratosphere, the mesosphere, the thermosphere and the exosphere. The temperature and amount of gases decreases in the upper layers of the atmosphere.

Exosphere
The exosphere is the outermost layer of our atmosphere. It is from 185 miles (300 km) above Earth's surface to 430 miles (700 km). It is also called the upper atmosphere.

Mesosphere
The mesosphere reaches from 30 miles (50 km) above the surface to 50 miles (80 km). Speeding chunks of space rock called meteors burn up in the mesosphere.

Thermosphere
The thermosphere is between 50 miles (80 km) and 185 miles (300 km) above the surface of earth. Here, heat from the sun is absorbed and bounced back.

Stratosphere
Above the troposphere is the stratosphere. It extends from seven miles (twelve kilometers) to 30 miles (50 km) above the surface.

Troposphere
The closest layer to Earth is the troposphere. It extends seven miles (twelve kilometers) above the surface. Weather occurs in the troposphere.

11

Holes in the Ozone

The layer of Earth's atmosphere called the stratosphere contains a chemical called ozone. Ozone sits in a band within the stratosphere, called the ozone layer. The ozone layer absorbs the sun's ultraviolet, or UV, rays and prevents them from reaching the surface. UV rays are very harmful if absorbed by the skin in large amounts, and can cause a disease called skin cancer and other health problems in people.

CFCs

In the past, people used large amounts of a chemical called chlorofluorocarbons, or CFCs, that destroyed the ozone layer. CFCs were ingredients in aerosol spray cans, the cooling materials in refrigerators and air conditioners, and in certain plastic foams. The release of great amounts of CFCs into the atmosphere caused holes to open up in the ozone layer.

On the road to a solution

Since the late 1980s, the use of CFCs in spray cans had been banned. Laws were passed to prevent the use of CFCs in refrigerators and air conditioners as well. Slowly, the ozone layer is beginning to repair itself, but it will still take many more years before the holes are completely fixed. Scientists, governments, manufacturers, and individuals worked together to bring about this change. The ozone depletion problem can be looked at as a partial success. Scientists and environmental organizations hope that similar steps can be taken to try and fix the problem of global warming, before it is too late.

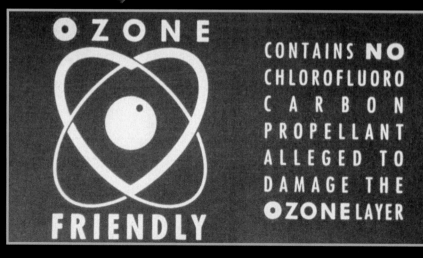

OZONE

CONTAINS **NO** CHLOROFLUORO CARBON PROPELLANT ALLEGED TO DAMAGE THE **OZONE** LAYER

FRIENDLY

Today, people still have to protect themselves from the sun's UV rays by wearing sunblock, loose clothing, and hats, and by limiting the amount of time they spend outdoors, especially on very sunny days.

Ozone holes step-by-step

1

The ozone layer is thinnest over the north and south poles.

2

In the past, people released CFCs through aerosol cans, refrigerator or air-conditioner coolant, and factories. The CFCs move through the atmosphere into the ozone layer.

3

CFCs continue to collect in the swirling winds that form at each pole during winter, when less sunlight hits the poles.

4

When the summer sun hits the CFCs, they combine with light in a process called photo-reaction, to thin the ozone layer.

5

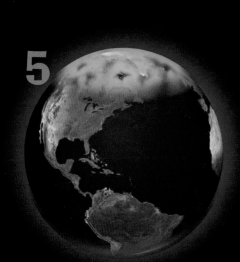

The holes grow smaller in the dark months of winter, but have not repaired completely.

Famous Disasters

Environmental disasters have caused loss of life, and have had long-lasting effects on land, air, and water. Unlike disasters that occur because of natural causes, in all of these instances of "famous" environmental disasters, human behavior and error were responsible.

Bhopal chemical explosion

Bhopal, India, is the site of one of the worst environmental disasters. In 1984, a huge explosion in a plant owned by an American chemical company sent an enormous cloud of poisonous gas over the area. More than 8,000 people died as a result of the chemical leak, and up to 500,000 people suffered very serious injuries. Scientific research suggests that survivors of the disaster may pass health problems to their children because their bodies have absorbed so many **toxins**. Soil and drinking water are still contaminated in Bhopal 20 years after the accident. Investigations into how this terrible environmental disaster happened suggests that the plant's operators "cut corners" in their safety inspections and tried to save money by using poor equipment and materials.

(above, left) People still live around the *pesticide* plant in Bhopal, India, where the poisonous gas leak took place, even though the land is now contaminated.

(insert) This woman was blinded because of the poisonous gas leak in Bhopal.

Chernobyl nuclear disaster

In 1986, a power plant in Chernobyl, present-day Ukraine, saw the worst **nuclear power** accident in history. Workers had been disregarding safety procedures, and a massive explosion occurred at one of the four nuclear **reactors**, blowing the lid off the reactor and sending a huge fireball into the air. Thirty people were killed immediately. High levels of **radiation** leaked into the atmosphere, water, and soil. In nearby areas, many people suffered from cancer, and in the ten years following the accident, more than 300,000 people were evacuated, or forced to leave their homes. In all, about a million people were affected by the radiation.

1986

(below) The remains of the fourth reactor in front of the chimney, at the nuclear power plant after the explosion in Chernobyl.

(inset) This piglet was born one year after the explosion on a farm 40 miles (65 km) away from Chernobyl. Radiation caused deformities in people and animals born after the accident.

Exxon Valdez oil spill

In 1989, a huge supertanker called the Exxon Valdez was attempting to enter the Pacific Ocean through Prince William Sound in Alaska, when it smashed into a rocky reef. The hole torn in the ship allowed more than eleven million gallons (42 million liters) of oil to spill into the water. The oil spread, moved along by choppy waters, and ended up covering more than 1,500 miles (2,400 km) of the Alaskan shoreline. Thousands of birds died from swallowing oil-poisoned water, because oil seeped into their skin, or because their oil-covered feathers could not keep them warm. Sea otters, salmon, harbor porpoises, sea lions, several types of whales, and herring were also affected. People in the area, especially many Native Americans who lived in fishing villages, were also affected, because the spill killed an important source of food for them, and because their chances of making a living through fishing were greatly reduced.

(above) A sea otter coated in oil tries to swim away from the disaster.

(below) Tugboats attempt to free the Exxon Valdez from Blight Reef, on which it was grounded.

Water pollution in history

Polluted water sources are often in the news as a major sources of environmental damage, but people have been polluting water with waste from industries and homes for many centuries. In **Roman times**, people tossed garbage and human waste directly into the Tiber River, to the point that the river became so polluted, the citizens of Rome had to look to other water sources for their drinking water. In the **Middle Ages**, farmers dumped agricultural waste into rivers, and people often tossed their garbage directly into water. Some **historians** believe that the unclean drinking water that resulted was a major factor in the spread of the Bubonic Plague, a widespread disease often called the Black Death, that killed millions of Europeans during this time. In **Renaissance** times, early water scientists noted that waste from leather tanning shops and metal manufacturing poisoned water and made it undrinkable.

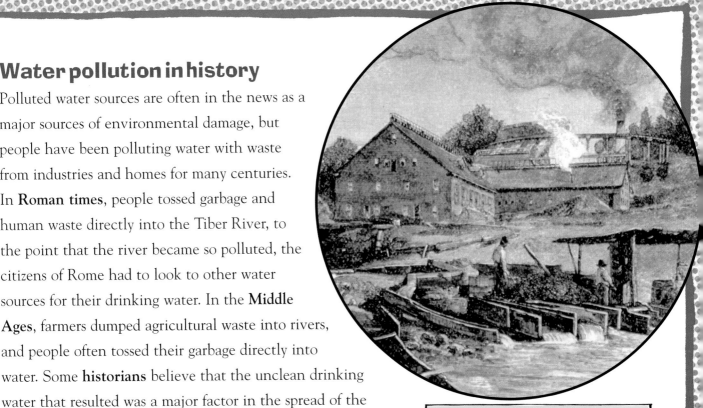

(above) Since ancient times, people have dumped waste into water sources without realizing the pollution it caused.

London smog

The London Smog Disaster happened in December 1952, in London, England. At that time, most people heated their homes by burning coal. As a result of unusually cold weather, people burned more coal than usual, releasing a chemical called sulphur dioxide into the air, which mixed with low-lying fog to create smog. The air pollution was responsible for about 4,000 deaths. After the incident, laws were passed to stop heating homes with coal.

Children are advised to get indoors during smog.

War on the Environment

During wars, chemicals have been used to kill plant life, to make it difficult for enemies to harvest crops for food, and to remove an enemy's ability to hide in forests. Explosives used in wars have left large areas of land unable to be used by people for agriculture and settlement.

FALLOUT SHELTER

Agent Orange

During the war in Vietnam in the 1960s and 1970s, the United States sprayed "Agent Orange," a herbicide, or plant-killing chemical, over large areas of Vietnam. The chemical was sprayed to removed foliage and expose the hiding spots of enemy soldiers. An estimated 17 million gallons (70 million liters) of Agent Orange was used. Agent Orange had a terrible effect on human life, and continues to do so today. People exposed to the chemicals suffer from several serious health problems, including cancer, deformities, higher rates of infant death, and **brain disorders**. Agent Orange hit the environment especially hard. Forests and large numbers of wild animals were completely wiped out. The destruction of forests has meant that water cannot be absorbed by the soil after rainfall. This has led to floods and droughts that have destroyed agricultural land. Widespread **erosion** has blocked rivers and streams, also leading to floods.

During World War II, countries around the world stockpiled massive amounts of ammunition, such as these mustard gas containers.

Landmines

Landmines are explosives buried just below the ground. They do not explode on impact, but blow up when a person or animal steps on them. Around the world, landmines have had a terrible effect on innocent people and animals who have come into contact with them. Landmines have weakened soil, leading to erosion and **metal pollution** in water. They have also made large areas of land unusable for agriculture.

Munitions dumping

In many instances, the end of war has marked the beginning of an environmental disaster in the world's oceans. Munitions dumping occurs when warring nations dump large amounts of "left over" weapons and explosives into the water. This can have a terrible effect on marine life, as plants, fish and other sea animals are exposed to pollution from metals. Decades after World War II, there is still a great deal of concern about how the pollution caused by munitions dumping in the northern parts of the Atlantic Ocean has effected fish and other marine life.

Soldiers sometimes destroy resources so that others cannot use them. During the 1991 Persian Gulf War, Iraqi soldiers set fire to oil fields, releasing poisonous gas into the air.

Anti-nuclear movement

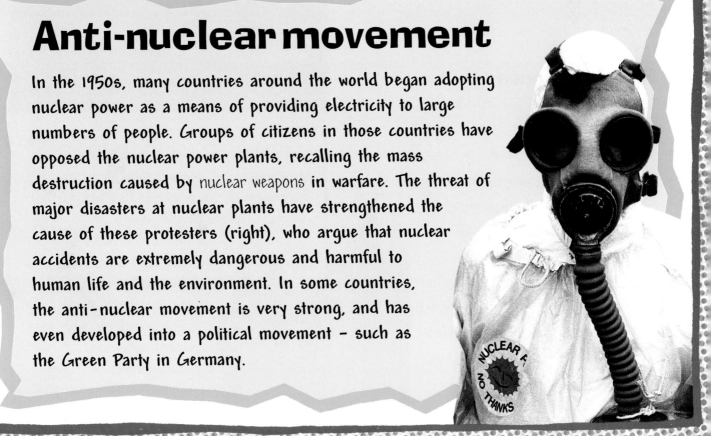

In the 1950s, many countries around the world began adopting nuclear power as a means of providing electricity to large numbers of people. Groups of citizens in those countries have opposed the nuclear power plants, recalling the mass destruction caused by nuclear weapons in warfare. The threat of major disasters at nuclear plants have strengthened the cause of these protesters (right), who argue that nuclear accidents are extremely dangerous and harmful to human life and the environment. In some countries, the anti-nuclear movement is very strong, and has even developed into a political movement - such as the Green Party in Germany.

Disaster Alert!

Many organizations have members who devote their time to monitoring the environment. They try to make sure that environmental disasters do not happen. Environmental scientists help them in their work. Environmental scientists are people who take information about the environment, such as measuring soil, water, and air samples for pollution levels, and then use that information to recommend ways of changing environmental practices.

On guard

Sometimes, environmental organizations act as "watchdogs" to make sure industries are using environmentally safe practices in manufacturing and disposing of waste. In other cases, they work with governments to make laws that force individuals and companies to act in ways that benefit the environment. Some groups stage protests to show their disagreement with various environmental practices of governments or companies.

Pick your cause

There are different types of environmental organizations. Some are developed and paid for by governments to improve environmental conditions for their people. In the United States, the Environmental Protection Agency, or EPA, is one such organization. Others are run as private, **profit**-making companies. Still others are run as not-for-profit organizations, which means they rely on money donated, or given to them, by people, companies, and government, to do their work.

(above) One well-known example of an environmental organization is Greenpeace, an international group that works to make people aware of environmental problems.
(top and left) Greenpeace stages events to get media attention, such as placing these styrofoam fish in Argentina's most polluted river.

(left) Indonesians protect themselves from breathing in smog produced by waste gases on this busy highway.

(below) Environmental scientists in the lab test soil and water samples.

Monitoring acid rain levels

Many companies and governments have started to develop tests for measuring the acid levels in rain water, lakes, and rivers. Scientists use a measurement called the pH scale, on which low numbers indicate high concentrations of acid, and high numbers indicate low concentrations. By measuring rain or lake waters and then testing them in labs for their pH levels, scientists can tell if the water cycle has been contaminated by acid rain – and can work to force local industries to cut down on the pollutants they emit into the atmosphere.

A better future?

The Kyoto **Accord** was an attempt by leaders of powerful countries to cut down on greenhouse gas buildup, by the year 2012. Some countries, such as Canada, signed the agreement to help reduce greenhouse gases. Other countries, such as the U.S.A. and Australia, agreed with the ideas behind the accord, but could not get their governments to work toward the agreement.

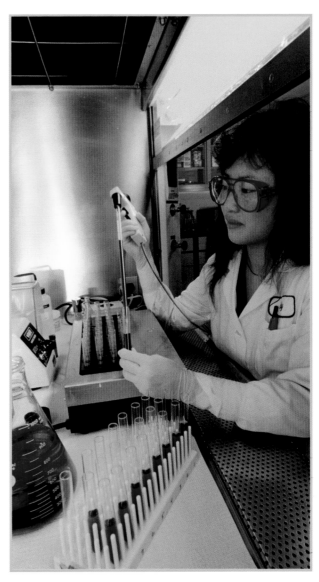

Protecting Earth

Making sure our environment stays healthy for years to come is something that needs to start close to home. Cleaning up a local park, or working around home and school to make sure that cans, plastics, and paper items end up in recycling containers, goes a long way toward saving our planet.

Recycling

In most communities in North America, there are recycling programs in place. These programs are supported by private companies and by governments, who encourage people to "re-use" and "recycle" items made of paper, plastic, and metal. The practice of re-using and recycling plastic and glass bottles, soda cans, and paper saves the materials these objects are made from, and the energy needed to destroy the old objects and make new ones.

(right) Recycle items made of glass, metal, plastic, and paper.

Turn out the lights!

The electricity we use to power microwaves, light our houses, and watch TV is produced in power plants that burn fossil fuels. If people make use of energy-efficient lightbulbs, turn on only the lights they need, and even cut down on their TV-watching, they will be doing a lot to reduce global warming because less fossil fuels will be needed to produce that electricity. These might seem like tiny steps to take, but if everyone did them, the effect could be enormous.

(left) This student in Kenya, Africa, is planting trees as part of a school project.

Do your part!

There are many things you can do around your home and school to protect the environment. Here are just a few of them:

* Recycle glass, cans, plastic, and paper whenever possible.
* Put garbage in trash cans. Do not litter!
* Try to avoid taking the car when you can walk, ride a bike, or use some other form of transportation that does not use gas.
* Plant trees - they absorb carbon dioxide from the air.
* Buy products designed to save energy. These come with special labels so you can tell that a stereo, computer, or VCR is an energy-saver.
* Whenever possible, save electricity by turning out unnecessary lights, TVs, computers, etc.
* Avoid spraying lawns and gardens with pesticides. Pesticides contain harmful chemicals that can poison water and soil.
* Use environmentally-friendly cleaning supplies. These cleaners often have ingredients that are bio-degradable.

* Get together with family and friends at school or at home to talk about ways you can help the environment. Sharing ideas is the best way to protect the natural world around us.

Emissions control

People have long been concerned that with so many vehicles on roads, the pollution caused by waste gases will lead to an overload of smog in the atmosphere. Scientists have had a hard time developing vehicles that are cheap enough for most people to use, and that use energy efficiently. Recently, engineers have come up with "hybrid" cars that use both electric and gas power to run (right). These cars use less gas and cause less pollution - a great combination that will likely mean that hybrids will become more and more common around the world.

Aftermath

Some of the damage environmental disasters cause will never be repaired, but humans still have the responsibility to try and clean up the affected areas. Recovery efforts are often dangerous, because workers are exposed to contamination as they try to restore plant and animal life, and detoxify poisoned soil and water.

Cleaning up an oil spill

Cleaning up an oil spill involves cleaning the water and helping plant and animal life recover from the damage. Large oil spills, such as the 1989 Exxon Valdez disaster, take many years and several billion dollars to clean up. Rescue and recovery agencies use cleanup barges, or large flat-bottomed boats, that have huge barrels on their decks. The barrels have hoses attached to them that crew members place in the water to suck up the oil from the water's surface.

Other cleanup devices include booms, or floating barriers that prevent the spread of oil on water; boats that skim spilled oil from the water surface called skimmers; and various large sponge-like devices, called sorbents, which soak up the oil, and are then taken away and disposed of. Oil-spill cleanup crews use different chemicals to break down the oil, and a process called in-situ burning, in which oil sitting on top of water is burned off.

Shorelines affected by oil spills must also be cleaned. Workers use high-powered hot water hoses to clean the oil from these rocks.

Cleaning animals after an oil spill is a time consuming job. It requires hundreds of volunteers to clean each animal individually. Unfortunately, some chemicals used to clean the water are poisonous to sea birds, who try to groom their feathers and end up swallowing the oil and the chemicals.

Saving wildlife

Recovery workers try to save birds, fish, and other animals that have suffered from being coated in oil. Scientists round up as many oil-soaked birds as possible, dunk the birds, one-by-one, in a mixture of soap and water, and scrub the feathers clean with a brush. Many birds die from the stress it takes to do this. Other animals can be cleaned in the same way, and moved to uncontaminated areas. Often, authorities in areas where oil spills occur will make it illegal to fish there, even after the oil has been cleaned from the water, so that fish populations can grow back to a healthy size.

A sorbent boom helps prevent oil from spreading.

Re-stocking the lake

Factories often dumped **toxic waste** directly into North American lakes until the 1960s, when laws were passed to prevent this practice. The fish and other animals that lived in many of these lakes died because of the poisoned water and contaminated **sediment** on the lake bottom. This type of contamination also meant it was very risky for humans to use the lakes, both as a source of food, and for recreation such as swimming. Luckily, scientists began developing ways to re-introduce fish back into contaminated lakes after cleaning them up.

Re-stocking a contaminated lake involves many steps. First, scientists take measurements of the water, the soil at the lake bottom, and the fish themselves, to see what harmful chemicals exist in the lake, and how much of these chemicals are present. The contaminated sediment is removed from the bottom of the lake, using large machinery, and disposed of in a safe site. New chemicals are often added to the lake's water, to "clean up" the water by cancelling out the effects of the poisonous chemicals. All contaminated fish and plants are removed from the lake, and destroyed so that they cannot return to re-introduce contaminants into the lake. New fish are put into the lake, and are continually monitored to make sure they remain healthy, and are safe for humans to catch and eat. In many cases, scientists try to introduce plants that absorb toxic chemicals and help keep the lake clean.

(above) Scientists who test lake water wear protective suits.

(below) This scientist is taking a sample from a lake to test the pollution level of the water.

26

Replanting a forest

Tree-replanting in areas devastated by too much logging is a difficult process. The elimination of trees may have led to valuable soil being washed away, without the tree roots to keep it in place. Foresters need to decide if they should re-plant using just one kind of tree, or several. Depending on soil conditions, they need to decide whether planting new trees from seeds, or from small trees that will grow into much larger ones - called seedlings - is the best course of action.

(top) Sometimes, logging activities are not properly managed to ensure the survival of a forest. Today, many logging companies and environmental organizations plant trees after an area has been cleared.

The city of Moriupol is the Ukraine's most polluted city. Together with the government, the city set up a program to find out the relationship between children's health problems and air, water, and soil pollution from industries, such as the factory in the background of this picture. Pollution often has a greater effect on young children and the elderly.

27

Planet Survival

Many parts of South America, Africa, and Asia are covered by tropical rainforests. Rainforests exist in areas that are very warm and have large amounts of rainfall. These forests are home to an incredible number of plants, trees, and animals.

Busy forests

Scientists estimate that from 50 to 90 percent of the world's living species make their homes in rainforests, and about one half of all the growing wood on Earth originates there, even though the forests themselves take up only about seven percent of the Earth's land. Hundreds of thousands of different types of birds, monkeys, and insects live on top of the rainforest's branches, or canopy. Many medicines we use today come from plants and trees that exist only in rainforests.

For many centuries, indigenous, or native, peoples living in rainforests have used the plants that grow there as an important source of medicine.

Oxygen factories

Trees create oxygen in a process called photosynthesis. They also absorb carbon dioxide, the gas believed to be mainly responsible for global warming. The abundance of trees and other plant life in rain forests is beneficial to the environment.

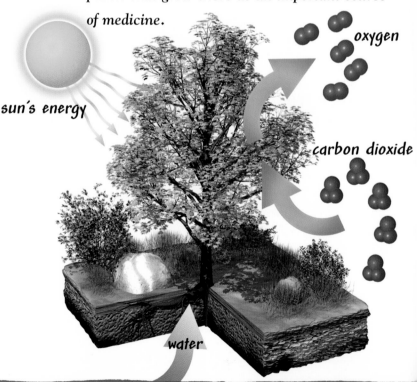

sun's energy

oxygen

carbon dioxide

water

Slash-and-burn

Slash-and-burn is a way of clearing land for growing crops that has been used for centuries in rainforests such as the Amazon, in South America. In slash-and-burn, all the vegetation in a large area of forest is cut down, or slashed, and set on fire. The ash from the burned trees and plants adds **nutrients** to the soil. The soil can only be used for a few years before the nutrients are used up and another area of forest burned. It takes about ten years or more for an area to recover. Slash-and-burn is not harmful to the environment until there are too many people practicing it and more and more forest has to be cleared. Often, there is little or no attempt by the people who practice slash-and-burn to replant the forests.

This African rainforest is being destroyed because too much of it is being cleared by slash-and-burn agriculture.

Overpopulation

Since humans first started burning wood, hunting animals, and harvesting plants for food, we have been interacting with our environment. When we start to use too much of what nature can give us, then environmental problems start to happen. Plants and animals have natural ways of replacing themselves, and keeping their populations healthy. Sometimes, people start to use them up them so quickly that they can not regrow fast enough. This happens especially quickly when the human population in an area grows rapidly, and people start to use up their natural resources faster than the resources can be replenished. Overpopulation, which means too many people living on the planet, is the leading cause of environmental depletion.

Recipe for Disaster

The following activity allows you to re-create an oil spill in miniature form. You will also be able to see how animal and plant life that lives in or near water is affected by a spill.

What you need:
* A large plastic or glass bowl
* Enough warm water to fill the bowl about half full
* A teaspoon of salt
* Approximately one cup of vegetable or olive oil
* A piece of fabric (wool or cotton)
* A small plastic or rubber ball

What to do:
1. Fill the bowl half full with water.

2. Add the salt and stir so that salt mixes thoroughly with water.

3. Gradually add oil, and stir gently. Observe how the oil spreads through the water. What patterns does it follow? How does it interact with the salt in the water?

4. Place fabric on top of the water, and leave it there for 5-10 minutes. What happens to the fabric when you remove it from the water?

5. Immerse the ball completely in the water and hold down for about 30 seconds. What happens to the ball?

What you will see:

The oil floats on top of the water. When you take the fabric out of the water, it is coated with a layer of oil and salt. When you let go of the ball, it floats to the surface of the water, and is coated with the oil/salt mixture. This gives you some idea of what happens to fish, birds, or water mammals who are covered with oil and salty water.

Try rinsing the cloth and the ball under warm water. Do you see the water form beads on top of the oil? Now try using a mild dish soap to clean them. With a bit of scrubbing, the oil should come off. Just imagine if it was a bird's feathers you were trying to scrub clean!

Glossary

acid rain Rain that is high in certain poisonous chemicals caused by air pollution

accord A formal agreement

bio-degradable Able to break down naturally

brain disorders Diseases caused by improper functioning of the brain

carbon dioxide A colorless, odorless gas produced when humans and animals breathe and when fossil fuels, are burned

chemicals Substances with a specific makeup that can be mixed with others to produce a desired effect

condensation A process in which hot gases cool and turn to liquid

contaminated Polluted, or made impure

deformities Not the usual shape

depletion The gradual using up of something

detoxify To remove poisons, or toxins

drought A period when little or no rain falls

environmental organizations Groups of people who work together to protect the natural world

erosion The gradual wearing away of soil or rock

fossil fuels Coal, oil, and gas burned for fuel energy

historians People who study the past

media Newspapers, radio reports, and TV news

metal pollution Being made dirty or poisonous from metals, such as mercury

Middle Ages The period in European history between 500 A.D. and 1500 A.D.

mythical Not real

nuclear power Energy created by splitting the nucleus, or center, of atoms, or tiny bits of matter

nuclear weapons Explosives that get their power from the splitting of atoms

nutrients Substances that make something healthy

oil spill The accidental release of oil into a body of water

pesticides Chemicals used to kill pests

photo-reaction The result of light on chemicals

photosynthesis The process in which green plants use sunlight, water, and carbon dioxide to make food

pollutants Substances that pollute, or make dirty

profit Money made from selling or buying

protesters People who take action to show their displeasure at rallies, parades, or events

radiation A strong stream of energy waves

reactor A device in which atoms are split

Renaissance The period in European history that marks the change from the medieval to modern world, from about 1300 to 1600 A.D.

Roman times The period of history from about 300 B.C. to 450 A.D. when Rome's empire covered most of Europe and the Middle East

sediment A build up of dirt over time

seep To trickle down slowly

smog A thick mixture of smoke and fog

toxic waste Poisonous leftovers

toxins Poisonous substances, caused by pollution

waste gasses Harmful gases that come from burning fossil fuels

Index

1 2 3 4 5 6 7 8 9 0   Printed in the U.S.A.   0 9 8 7 6 5 4